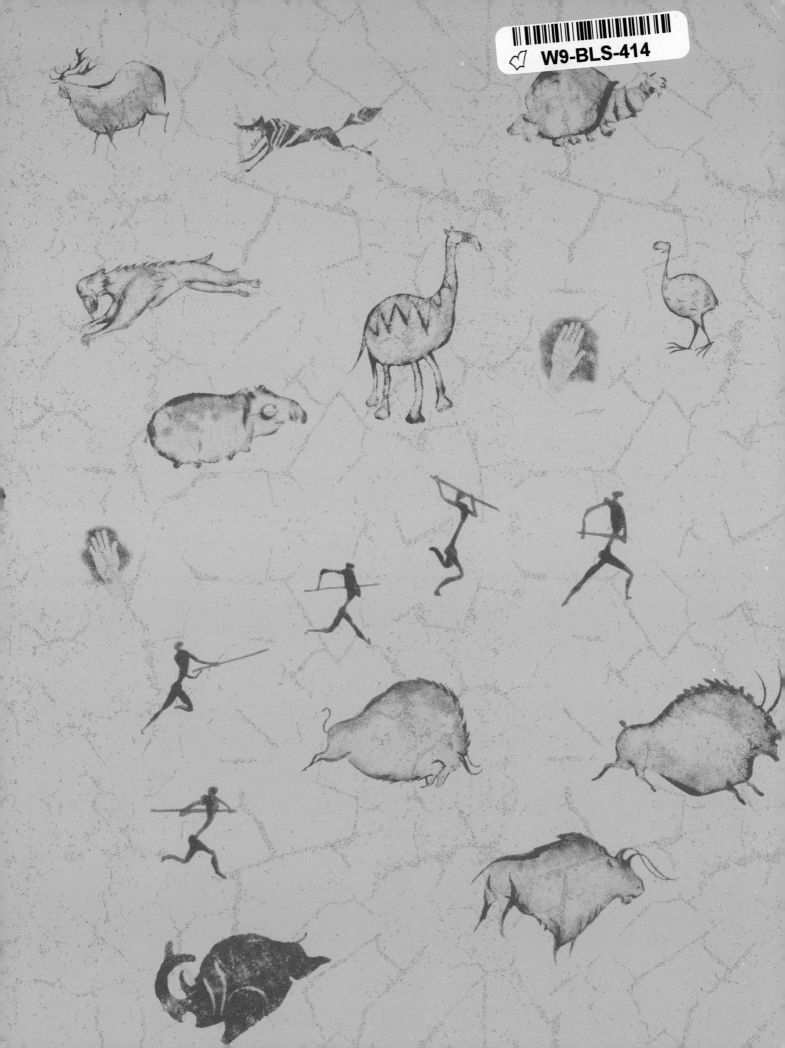

THE CLASSIC STORYBOOK

ADAPTED BY NANCY KRULIK

HarperEntertainment

An Imprint of HarperCollins*Publishers*

HarperCollins books are available at special quantity discounts for bulk purchases for sales promotions, premiums, or fund-raising. For information please call or write: Special Markets Department, HarperCollins Publishers Inc., 10 East 53rd Street, New York, NY 10022. Telephone: (212) 207-7528. Fax: (212) 207-7222.

ISBN 0-06-621439-4

HarperCollins®, 📖®, and HarperEntertainment™ are trademarks of HarperCollins Publishers Inc.

First printing: February 2002

Visit HarperEntertainment on the World Wide Web at www.harpercollins.com

10 9 8 7 6 5 4 3

PROLOGUE

Long, long ago, when woolly mammoths and saber-toothed tigers roamed the land, a deep freeze settled over the earth. As the unbearable cold spread across the plain, an ancient squirrel-like creature held tight to his only acorn. Food was scarce, and the scrat wanted to be sure that his meal was safe. He tried desperately to bury it, but the ice was too thick.

The tiny scrat jumped up and down on his acorn, attempting to stomp it into the ground. This forced a crack in the ice—not just a small crack, but a rift that spread across the ice plain and all the way up a tall glacier. The scrat watched with fear as giant chunks of ice careened from one glacier to the next, knocking them down like dominoes. Suddenly, frozen rocks were falling as far as the eye could see.

The Ice Age had begun.

"Look at this crowd," an impatient, short-snouted creature moaned as he stood in a southbound traffic jam along the migration trail. "I knew we should have left early."

"Fall's never been this cold, dear," his wife said. "Everybody feels it."

Then, just as the restless animal thought things couldn't get any worse, a huge woolly mammoth named Manfred lumbered through the crowd, heading *north* on the trail. He was causing an even bigger traffic jam.

Manfred was not the only creature heading the wrong way that morning. A slovenly sloth named Sidney had been fast asleep in a tree. Now the heavy thuds of the migrating animals' footsteps woke him up. As he slipped from his perch, he saw an overeager female sloth heading right for him. Oh, no! It was Sylvia. Sid moaned. One way or another, conversations with her always turned to "commitment"—something Sid was definitely not into!

But today good luck was with him. Before Sylvia could force Sid into heading south with her, a crowd of glyptodons came waddling by. The herd of mammals was moving in Sylvia's direction. With a little nudge from Sid, Sylvia was swept away by them. Sid was relieved to have slipped out of this commitment at least for a while.

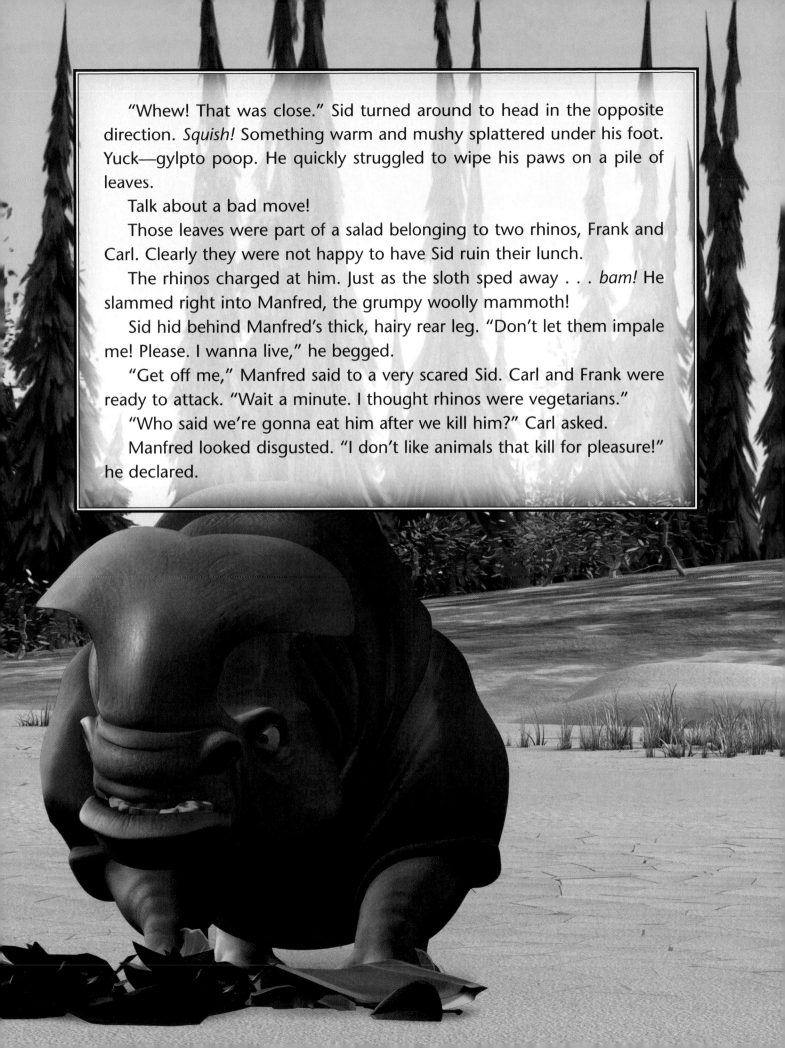

"Whew! That was close." Sid turned around to head in the opposite direction. *Squish!* Something warm and mushy splattered under his foot. Yuck—gylpto poop. He quickly struggled to wipe his paws on a pile of leaves.

Talk about a bad move!

Those leaves were part of a salad belonging to two rhinos, Frank and Carl. Clearly they were not happy to have Sid ruin their lunch.

The rhinos charged at him. Just as the sloth sped away . . . *bam!* He slammed right into Manfred, the grumpy woolly mammoth!

Sid hid behind Manfred's thick, hairy rear leg. "Don't let them impale me! Please. I wanna live," he begged.

"Get off me," Manfred said to a very scared Sid. Carl and Frank were ready to attack. "Wait a minute. I thought rhinos were vegetarians."

"Who said we're gonna eat him after we kill him?" Carl asked.

Manfred looked disgusted. "I don't like animals that kill for pleasure!" he declared.

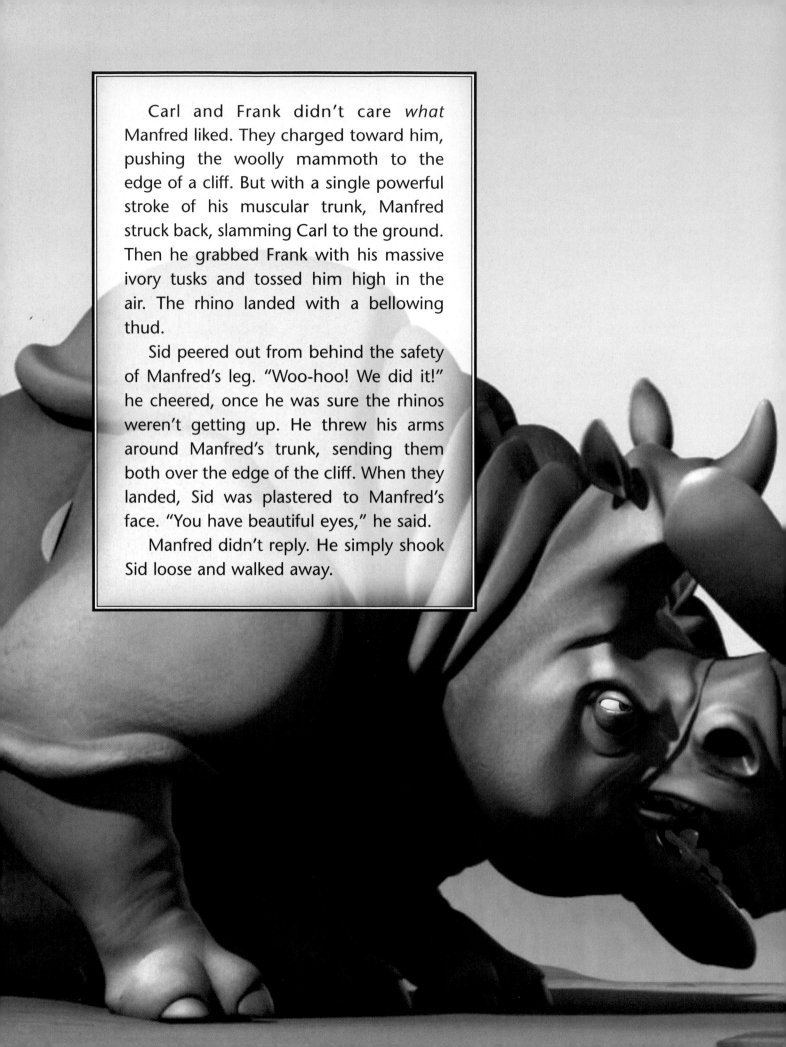

Carl and Frank didn't care *what* Manfred liked. They charged toward him, pushing the woolly mammoth to the edge of a cliff. But with a single powerful stroke of his muscular trunk, Manfred struck back, slamming Carl to the ground. Then he grabbed Frank with his massive ivory tusks and tossed him high in the air. The rhino landed with a bellowing thud.

Sid peered out from behind the safety of Manfred's leg. "Woo-hoo! We did it!" he cheered, once he was sure the rhinos weren't getting up. He threw his arms around Manfred's trunk, sending them both over the edge of the cliff. When they landed, Sid was plastered to Manfred's face. "You have beautiful eyes," he said.

Manfred didn't reply. He simply shook Sid loose and walked away.

"Whoa! We make a great team!" Sid called after him. "What d'ya say we just head south together?"

"Great! Yeah! Jump on my back and relax the whole way!"

"Wow, really?"

"No," Manfred snapped back.

"Wait, aren't you going south?" Sid asked, running after him.

Manfred didn't answer. He just kept walking north.

Sid considered his options. It was awfully cold up where Manfred was heading. But when Carl and Frank recovered, they were going to be *very* upset.

"That whole south thing is way overrated," Sid finally declared. "The heat, the crowds—who needs it?"

"You just want a bodyguard so you don't become somebody's side dish," Manfred countered.

"You're a very shrewd mammal," Sid told his new traveling companion.

Meanwhile, as Sid and Manfred were heading north, a pack of saber-toothed tigers was plotting an attack of their own. Soto, the leader of the pack, was furious with a tribe of humans who had moved into his territory. The humans had killed half of his tigers and were now wearing their skins to keep warm. He wanted revenge.

Soto sat on a cliff and watched from above as Runar, the human tribe's leader, played with his infant son, Roshan. "Isn't it nice he'll be joining us for breakfast?" Soto said to Diego, his second-in-command.

"It wouldn't be breakfast without him," Diego answered. "Let's show that human what happens when he messes with sabers."

"Alert the troops," Soto said to Diego. "We attack at dawn. Bring me that baby, Diego, and bring it alive."

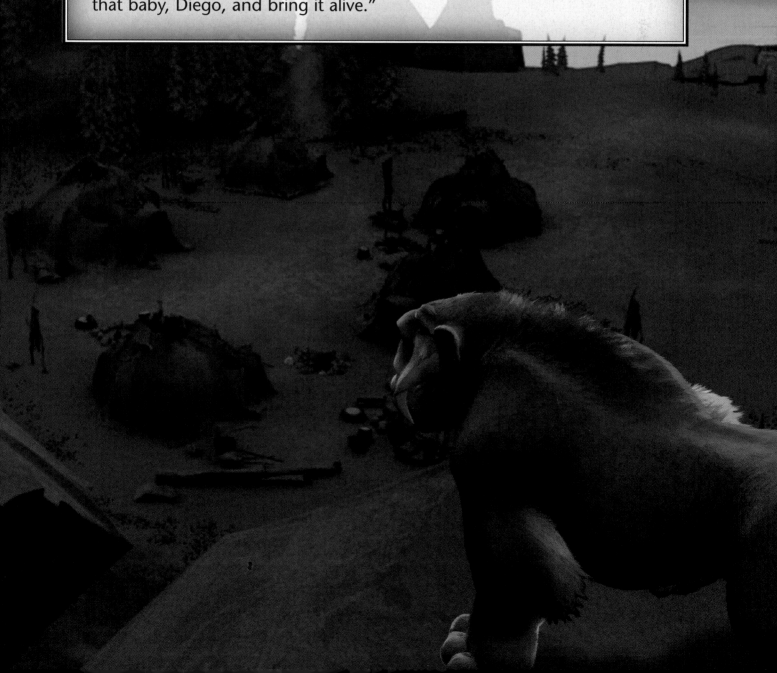

Later that evening Manfred collected some branches and brush from the plain to build a shelter. Sid followed lazily, dragging one dead branch behind him.

"That's your shelter?"

"Hey, you're a big guy, you got a lot of wood. I'm a little guy."

"You got half a stick."

"Yeah, but with my little stick and my highly evolved brain . . . ow!" He poked himself in the eye. "I shall create fire."

Two hours later Sid was still rubbing two sticks together when it started to hail. Manfred was protected in his sturdy lean-to. "Any chance I could squeeze in there, Manny, ol' pal?"

But Manny was fast asleep. Disheartened, Sid tried to shield himself under Manny's tail as the hail pounded down all around him.

The tigers attacked the human camp at dawn. The surprise raid caught the tribe off guard. They fought hard, but the tigers were too powerful.

Nadia, Runar's wife, raced through the campsite clutching her son, Roshan. Diego was hot on her trail. He chased her to a cliff overlooking a thundering waterfall. Nadia knew if she stayed on the cliff, the tiger would surely kill her *and* her baby. If she jumped, at least Roshan's life might be spared.

Diego watched, wide-eyed, as mother and baby disappeared over the cliff. He had to find the child—alive.

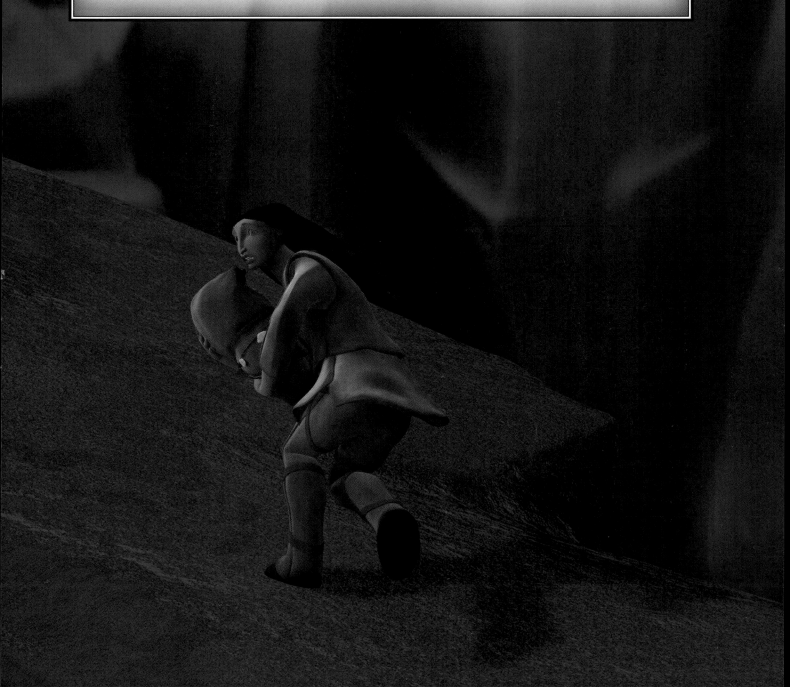

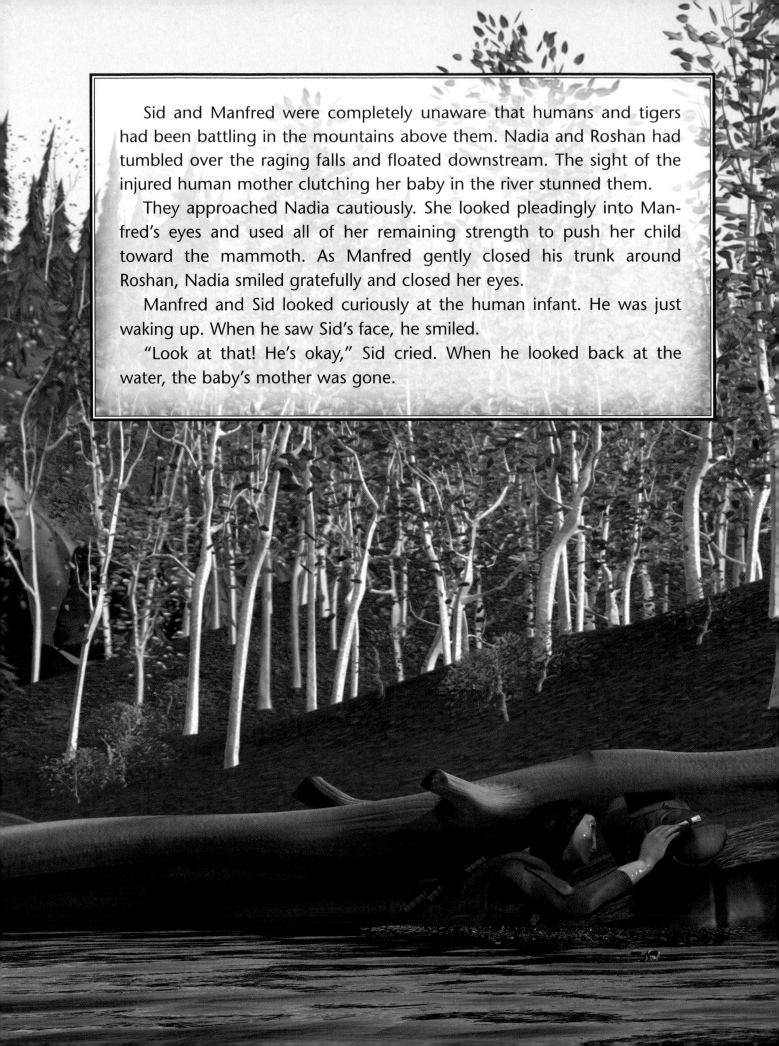

Sid and Manfred were completely unaware that humans and tigers had been battling in the mountains above them. Nadia and Roshan had tumbled over the raging falls and floated downstream. The sight of the injured human mother clutching her baby in the river stunned them.

They approached Nadia cautiously. She looked pleadingly into Manfred's eyes and used all of her remaining strength to push her child toward the mammoth. As Manfred gently closed his trunk around Roshan, Nadia smiled gratefully and closed her eyes.

Manfred and Sid looked curiously at the human infant. He was just waking up. When he saw Sid's face, he smiled.

"Look at that! He's okay," Sid cried. When he looked back at the water, the baby's mother was gone.

Manfred placed the baby on the ground with care and walked off.

Sid looked at him curiously. "Aren't you forgetting something?" he asked.

"No," Manfred replied.

"But you just saved him."

Manfred stared pointedly at Sid. "I'm still trying to get rid of the last thing I saved."

"But you can't leave him here."

Just then, Sid saw smoke rising from a hilltop in the distance. He picked up the baby. "That's his herd, right up the hill," he shouted. "We should return him."

Manfred sighed with exasperation. "Let's get something straight here, okay? There is no *we*!" he insisted. "There never was a *we*. In fact, without me, there wouldn't even be a *you*. Listen very carefully. I'm . . . *not* . . . going!" He gestured with his trunk to make his point.

"Fine, be a jerk," Sid declared. "I'll take care of him." He stuck the baby under one arm and began inching up the side of the sheer cliff as best he could. Unfortunately, sloths are not known for their climbing skills. He quickly lost his footing. As Sid stumbled, Roshan slid out of his grip. The baby tumbled through the air!

Sid grabbed onto the nearest rock, then stuck his paw out just in time to catch the baby by his diaper. Roshan was safe—but only for an instant. The stitching on the side of the diaper tore. Roshan slipped free and began to fall toward the ground.

In a flash, Diego leaped from a lower ledge on the cliff and snatched up Roshan in his teeth.

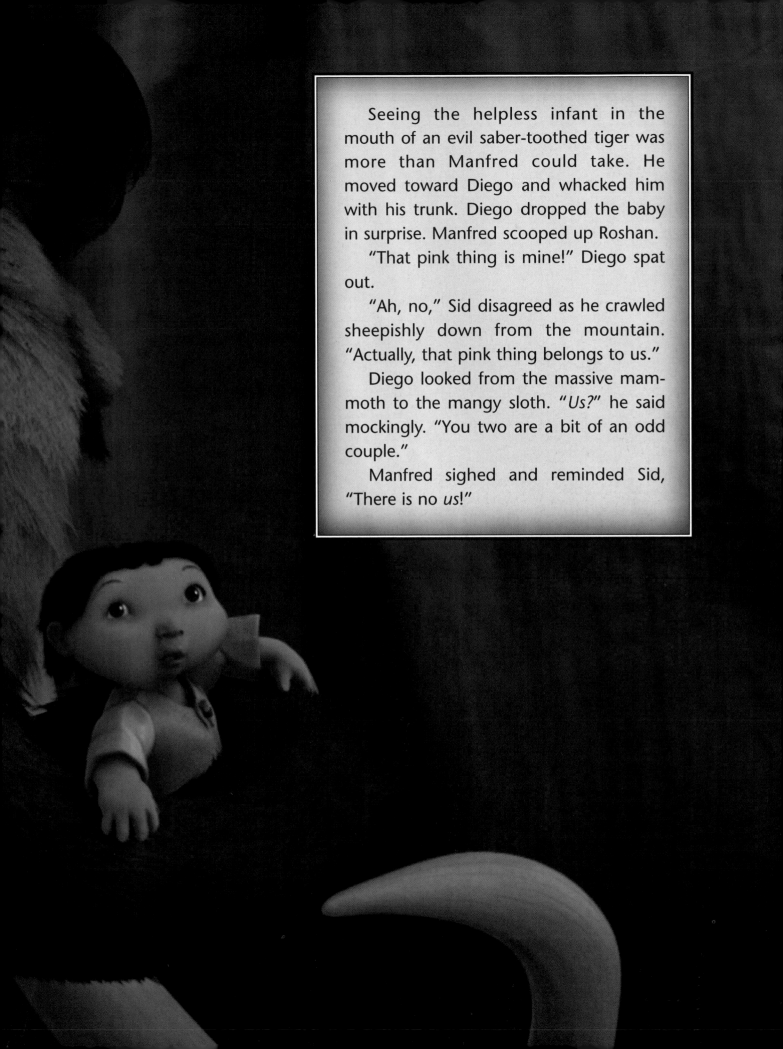

Seeing the helpless infant in the mouth of an evil saber-toothed tiger was more than Manfred could take. He moved toward Diego and whacked him with his trunk. Diego dropped the baby in surprise. Manfred scooped up Roshan.

"That pink thing is mine!" Diego spat out.

"Ah, no," Sid disagreed as he crawled sheepishly down from the mountain. "Actually, that pink thing belongs to us."

Diego looked from the massive mammoth to the mangy sloth. "*Us?*" he said mockingly. "You two are a bit of an odd couple."

Manfred sighed and reminded Sid, "There is no *us*!"

"The baby? Please. I was just returning him to his herd," Diego lied.

Manfred knew better. He wasn't turning the baby over to a vicious saber-toothed tiger. Of course, that left him with only one option. He would have to take the baby back to the human camp—with Sid.

But the humans were long gone, and Diego knew it. "They left this morning," he assured Manfred. The tiger yawned confidently, making sure Manfred and Sid saw his razor-sharp teeth. Obviously the saber-toothed tiger was not leaving this spot without that baby.

Manfred knew they needed Diego's tracking skills to lead them to the humans, so he agreed to let Diego come along, while *he and Sid* held on to the baby. Leading the way for these two wasn't what Diego had in mind, but at least he could keep an eye on the kid.

The mission would be tough. Diego had no idea *how* tough. Neither did Manfred or Sid. When Roshan began to cry, Sid tried to calm him down, but the slippery, squirming child kept howling at the top of his lungs.

Roshan's wailing seemed to get louder with every step they took. The animals tried everything to stop him—Sid even changed his dirty diaper! But the baby just kept crying.

Finally, Diego decided to take matters into his own paws. The tiger covered his eyes and moved his face closer to Roshan's. "Where's the baby?" he cooed. He uncovered his eyes and jumped toward Roshan. "There he is!"

But playing peekaboo with a tiger made the baby cry even harder.

"Stop it! You're scaring him," Manfred yelled, grabbing Roshan.

"I bet he's hungry," Sid said.

At the same time all three animals spotted a large melon sitting on the ground nearby. "Food!" they shouted. Manfred ran over to pick up the melon. As he did, a strange-looking creature called a dodo bird ran by and grabbed it from him. Sid, Manfred, and Diego chased the bird.

Roshan howled. There was no time to waste!

The trio followed the funny bird until they encountered an entire army of dodos.

Manfred asked them to return the melon he had found. "Junior's hungry."

"No way!" Dab, the head dodo, exclaimed. "This is our private stockpile for the Ice Age. Subarctic temperatures will force us underground for a million billion years."

Manfred laughed. "So you got three melons?"

"If you weren't smart enough to plan ahead, then doom on you!" cried Dab.

But it was doom on the dodos. Dab pounced on the first melon, accidentally shooting it to Roshan. An army of tae kwon dodos retrieved it and passed it over their shoulders from one dodo to the next, until the last dodo tossed it over a cliff!

Three dodos chased the second melon. But instead of saving it, the dodos *and* the melon fell into a pit of boiling water. As the last melon bounced back and forth between dodos, Sid managed to catch it, tackle a tower of dodos, and still land on his feet in front of Manfred, Diego, and Roshan. He did a victory dance, spiking the melon to the ground. *Splat!* Soon the only sound in the camp came from Roshan, who was happily munching on the squashed melon. *Mission accomplished.*

After Roshan's tasty dinner, it was time to set up camp for the night. As they slept, Zeke and Oscar, two tigers from Soto's pack, snuck up and hid in the bushes to check on Diego's progress. Diego was *not* happy to see them.

"Tracking down helpless infants too difficult for you?" Oscar whispered to Diego in a sarcastic tone. "Soto is getting tired of waiting."

"He said come back with the baby or don't come back at all," Zeke added.

Diego bared his teeth in a sinister grin. "I have a message for Soto. Tell him I'm bringing the baby, and tell him I'm bringing a . . . mammoth!" Diego moved aside so that Zeke and Oscar could see Manfred asleep with Roshan curled up in his trunk.

"Mmmm. Look at all that meat," Zeke remarked, licking his chops. "Let's get him!" He raced toward Manfred.

Diego stopped him in his tracks. "Not yet!" he insisted. "We'll need the whole pack to bring this mammoth down. Get everyone ready."

The next morning Manfred awoke early. He stretched his limbs wearily, then looked around for Roshan. But the baby was nowhere to be found.

Quickly, Manfred bounded over to Diego. The sleeping cat sprang to his paws.

"Where's the baby?" Manfred demanded.

"What do you mean 'where's the baby'?" Diego repeated with a nervous gulp. "You lost it?"

Manfred and Diego realized at the same time that Sid was missing, too! What was he up to?

Just as they had suspected, Roshan was with Sid. They were taking a relaxing mud bath along with two female sloths, Jennifer and Rachel, who thought Roshan was absolutely adorable.

"What's the matter with you?" Manfred asked Sid as he removed Roshan from the tub.

Sid jumped out and ran after Manfred. "Please, I'm begging you, I need him."

"What, a good-looking guy like you?" the mammoth joked. Manfred plunked Roshan down on a thick tree branch as Sid swaggered back to the tub alone. But by the time the sloth got there, the ladies were gone. In their place sat Carl and Frank! Sid wasn't sticking around to chat with them. They were still *steaming* mad.

In the distance, Sid could hear Roshan giggling and cooing.

"What are you looking at, bone bag?" Manfred asked. It was hard for him to imagine this little human baby growing up to be a great predator. "You're just a little patch of fur. No fangs. No claws. Just folds of skin wrapped in mush. What kind of threat are you?"

Roshan reached over to show him, yanking out the biggest nose hair he could grab onto. "Ow!" yelled Manfred. In a strange sort of way, Manfred was growing fond of Roshan.

Meanwhile, back at the hot tub, Sidney heard another familiar voice. It was Sylvia's. In an attempt to dash away, Sid smacked right into Diego. "Put me in your mouth," the sloth pleaded.

"Get away from me," Diego said. But Sid persisted. He bit the tiger on his paw. When Diego screamed with surprise, Sid slipped between his open jaws and played dead. But Sylvia was not fooled. She was just disgusted. "Eat him," she told Diego. For a moment Sid feared Diego might.

Sid, Manfred, Diego, and Roshan continued on their journey. The weather was turning colder now. Tall, icy glaciers surrounded them and a thick layer of snow covered the ground.

Diego walked ahead of the others. He noticed a tiger's pawprint in the snow. He quickly rubbed it out and made a human footprint in its place. He had to get the baby to Soto soon. He showed the footprint to the others and led them off in that direction.

A little while later Diego spotted real human footprints, then real humans! He couldn't let Sid or Manfred see them, too. He looked around and noticed a wide crevice running through a nearby glacier. He grinned in relief.

"Hey, great news! I found a shortcut," he called to Manfred as he pointed to the long, narrow channel that cut through the frozen ice. "If we slip through there, we can beat the humans to the pass and drop the baby off on their trail. If we go the long way, we might miss them."

Manfred looked at the crevice. It was narrow, jagged, and seemingly endless. "Through there? What do you take me for?" he demanded.

Before Diego could respond, Sid walked toward them. "Hey, guys, check it out!" He held two icicles on either side of his throat. He stumbled around, pretending that an icicle had pierced him through the neck.

Diego could tell Manfred had had it with Sid's antics. "This time tomorrow you could be a free mammoth," Diego tempted him.

Freedom seemed like a great idea. "Sid, the tiger found a shortcut," Manfred announced.

Sid gazed up at the huge mountain of ice above him. Just looking at it made him dizzy. "No, thanks. I choose life," he declared.

"Then I suggest you take the short-cut," Diego replied in a menacing tone.

"Are you threatening me?" Sid asked suspiciously.

Diego couldn't bear it anymore. "Move, sloth!" he ordered with a thundering roar.

The sound of Diego's voice echoed through the frozen mountains. The echo turned into a loud rumble, then the ground began to shake. Within seconds, an avalanche of snow and ice raced down the mountain—straight toward them!

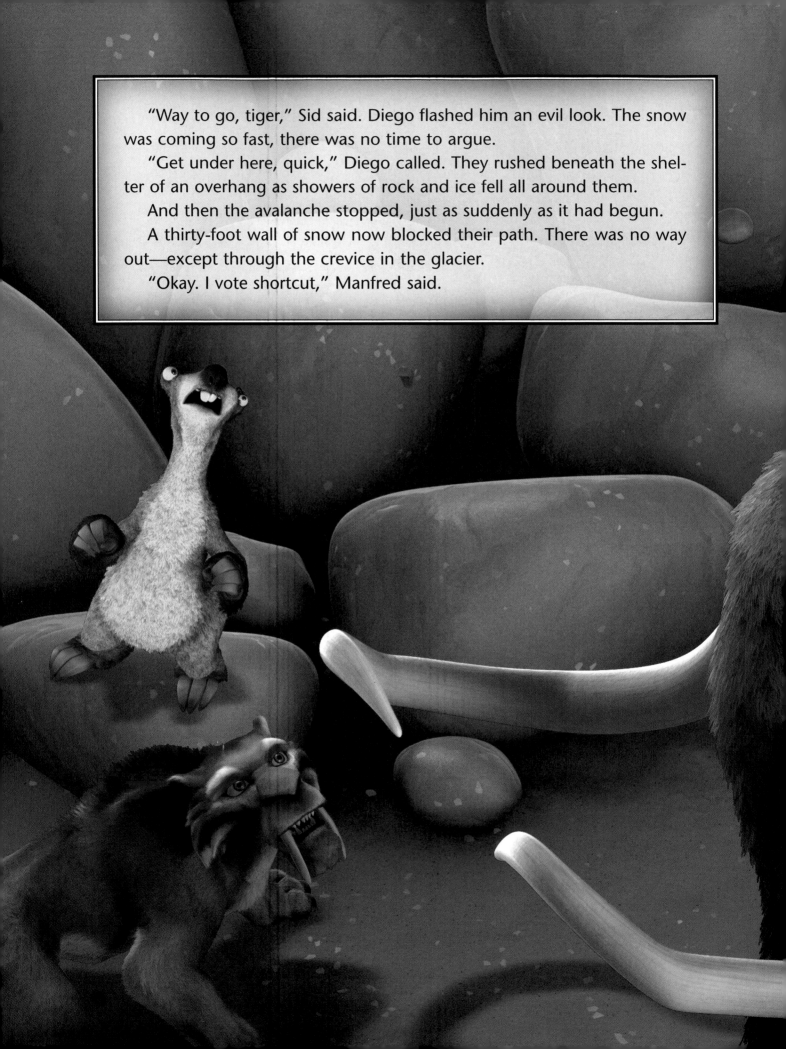

"Way to go, tiger," Sid said. Diego flashed him an evil look. The snow was coming so fast, there was no time to argue.

"Get under here, quick," Diego called. They rushed beneath the shelter of an overhang as showers of rock and ice fell all around them.

And then the avalanche stopped, just as suddenly as it had begun.

A thirty-foot wall of snow now blocked their path. There was no way out—except through the crevice in the glacier.

"Okay. I vote shortcut," Manfred said.

As he entered the space between the crevice, Sid looked up at the icy ceiling overhead. Shafts of light shone down on the path before him. Intricate web designs formed by cracks in the ice covered the surface of the walls. The place seemed almost magical.

As Sid turned a corner, he came face-to-face with a huge dinosaur, frozen forever in the ice. In another cave he noticed several wide-eyed, toothy figures, each one larger and more evolved than the last. The final figure looked remarkably like Sid.

Sid gulped and hurried to catch up with the others.

"Will you keep up, please?" Manfred ordered. "It's hard enough to keep track of *one* baby."

Without any of them noticing, Roshan climbed off Manfred's back and onto a slippery overhang. The next thing they knew, Roshan was shooting straight past them on a steep slide made of ice. Within seconds he had sailed into a tunnel and was completely out of sight.

Manfred, Sid, and Diego took off after him.

The slide was slick and cold. The animals picked up speed—whipping around turns, whooshing over ice bumps, and swirling through one ice tunnel after another.

Roshan squealed with joy as he bounced out of the animals' reach.

"Yeow!" Manfred screamed as he sailed sideways around a turn.

Sid shot out from yet another ice tunnel and landed with a thud on Manfred's shoulders. He grabbed the mammoth's huge tusks and tried to steer. Diego shot out from that same tunnel and landed clawsfirst on Manfred's huge rear end.

"Yeow!" Manfred shouted again as he and the others slipped down the slide.

A huge chunk of ice blocked the animals' path. *Slam!* They smashed right into it. Now the giant iceberg was under them. They rode it like a sled, faster and faster.

Sid was the first to reach Roshan. He grabbed the baby and held on tight. Suddenly, Sid's body left the ground. He and Roshan flew through the air. Finally, they crashed into a huge mound of snow with Diego and Manfred right behind them.

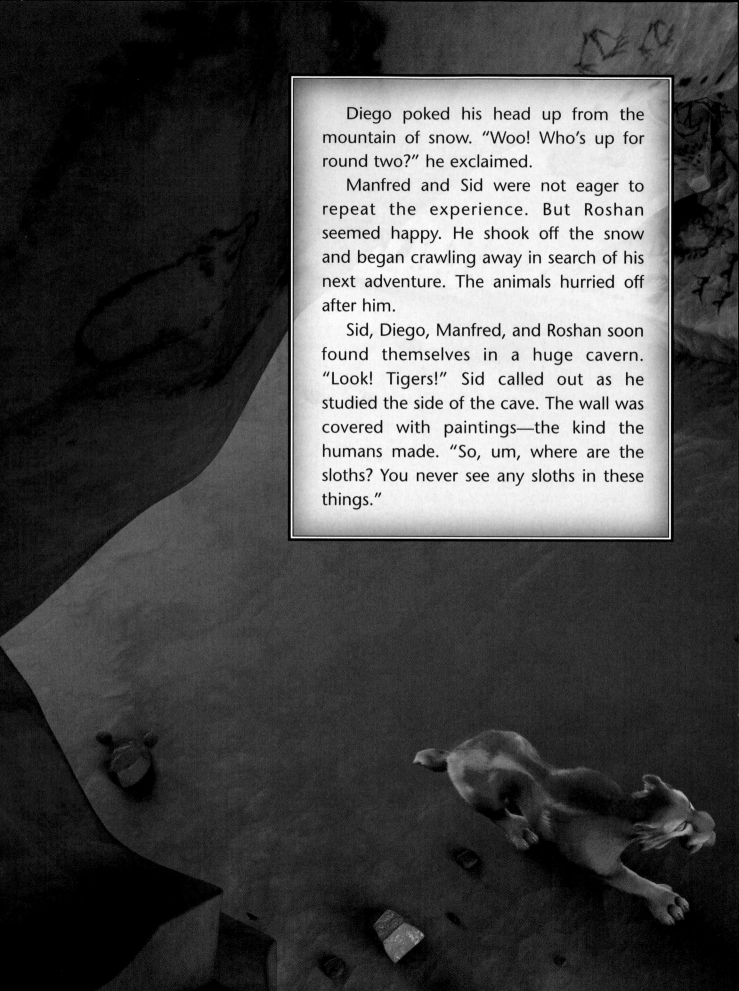

Diego poked his head up from the mountain of snow. "Woo! Who's up for round two?" he exclaimed.

Manfred and Sid were not eager to repeat the experience. But Roshan seemed happy. He shook off the snow and began crawling away in search of his next adventure. The animals hurried off after him.

Sid, Diego, Manfred, and Roshan soon found themselves in a huge cavern. "Look! Tigers!" Sid called out as he studied the side of the cave. The wall was covered with paintings—the kind the humans made. "So, um, where are the sloths? You never see any sloths in these things."

Sid went close to another drawing. "Look, Manny—a mammoth!"
Manfred rolled his eyes. "Ooo. Pinch me," he mumbled sarcastically.
"Hey, this fat one looks like you," Sid continued. "Look, he's playing with his kid. That's your problem. That's what mammoths are supposed to do. Find a she-mammoth, have a little baby mammoth—"
"Sid," Diego interrupted.

Manfred stood perfectly still and stared at the painting with wide, sad eyes. Diego came up beside him and studied the drawings closely, too. Beside the picture of the mammoth family playing was a drawing of humans with spears and another of the she-mammoth and her child being trapped and hunted by the humans.

Diego realized that this wasn't just any mammoth family. It was Manfred's family.

"Sid," Diego urged. "Shut up."

". . . oh," Sid said, finally understanding what Diego was trying to tell him.

There was utter silence in the cave. Nobody said anything. Manfred reached out his trunk to stroke the picture of his only child. Just as his trunk touched the image, it bumped Roshan's tiny hand. Roshan looked up at Manfred with innocent eyes, stumbling slightly with his arms held out straight, awaiting a hug. Manfred scooped him up with his trunk and held him close. He was determined to keep *this* baby safe.

All this emotion was too much for Sid. He sniffled sadly, then wiped a big green glob off the end of his nose and rubbed it onto Diego.

Manfred put Roshan on his back and left the cave without a word. Sid waddled out after him.

Diego lingered a moment longer, taking one last look at the paintings. He thought of the pain the hunters had caused Manfred. Now he was about to do the same.

While Roshan was in the comfort of the cave with his newfound friends, Roshan's dad, Runar, still searched the snow-covered valley for his son. The wolves tracking Roshan had lost his scent. It was time to give up the search. Runar clutched Roshan's necklace in the palm of his hand. Traces of the boy may have faded in the snow but never from Runar's heart.

As the animals left the cave, they caught a glimpse of a large volcano in the distance. "Well, would you look at that. The tiger actually did it! There's Half-Peak. How did I ever doubt you?" Manfred asked Diego.

Sid knew they were almost at Glacier Pass, where the humans were headed. "Did you hear that, little fellow?" he said to Roshan. "You're almost home."

Sid stood still for a moment and looked down at his paws. Suddenly, he noticed that the snow-covered land beneath him felt awfully warm.

"My feet are sweating," he mumbled with surprise.

"Do we have to get a news flash every time your body does something?" Diego hissed.

But Sid wasn't kidding. His paws were *really* hot. And to make matters worse, he could hear a low, deep rumbling coming from under his toes.

"Tell me that was your stomach," Manfred asked nervously.

"I'm sure it was just thunder," Sid replied in a shaky voice. "From under . . . ground?"

Suddenly, a blast of hot lava exploded from underneath the ice. *Boom! Boom! Boom!* Fountains of molten earth burst forth at a rapid pace. The sizzling liquid rock melted the snow, leaving large lakes in its place. Except for a few slim ice bridges spanning the ravine, the ground beneath the animals' paws was quickly disappearing.

"Run!" they all shouted.

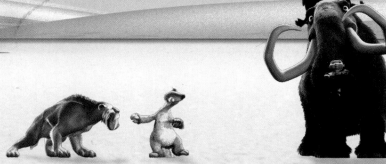

As they tried to make their way to more solid ground, a section of ice between Diego and Sid melted away. The tiger was left on a small island of his own. Quickly he leaped to the larger mound that held Manfred and Sid.

Sid looked from the melting ice beneath his paws to the solid ground that lay across a river of lava. "Wow! I wish I could jump like that."

Manfred kicked Sid hard from behind. "Wish granted," the mammoth declared. Then he jumped after Sid, landing beside him.

Diego leaped out and tried to join them, but he missed his mark and landed on a crumbling bridge. He dug his claws into the surface and struggled to pull himself up.

Manfred raced back to the bridge to help. "Hold on!" he called to Diego.

But Diego couldn't hold on any longer. His claws began to slip. Manfred stretched his trunk as far as he could to Diego, who grabbed hold of it with his claws. The mighty mammoth flung the tiger onto solid ground, saving him from the boiling lava lakes.

Crack! The bridge broke and Manfred fell, disappearing from their sight. But in no time at all another explosion of lava hurled him high up into the air. *Thud.* Manfred landed motionless in the snow near the others. Sid raced to his side. "Manny? Manny, are you okay? C'mon, say something," he begged. "*Anything!*"

"You're standing on my trunk," Manfred replied in a small, weak voice.

"Yay, you're okay!" Sid cheered.

"Why did you do that?" the tiger asked. "You could've died trying to save me."

"That's what you do in a herd," the mammoth explained simply. "You look out for each other."

"Well, thanks," Diego said, clearly uncomfortable. No one in his own pack had ever done anything like that for him before. It had always been every tiger for himself.

"We're the weirdest herd *I've* ever seen," Sid joked.

The animals found a place to take a much-needed rest at the top of the mountain. As Manfred kept an eye on Roshan, Sid drew a picture of a sloth.

"What are you doing?" Diego asked.

"Putting sloths on the map," Sid replied.

Manfred grabbed the rock from Sid and began to draw a more realistic-looking sloth.

"Make him rounder," cried Diego. "And stupider."

Sid snatched the rock back and was crossing out the chubby, pear-shaped sloth Manfred had drawn when sparks began to fly.

"I'm a genius," Sid shouted.

Before long he and Diego were bickering as usual in the glow of the warm, crackling fire Sid had built using the rock as flint.

"Hey, lovebirds, would you look at this," Manfred remarked. Roshan was standing on his own and trying to walk for the first time.

"Come here, you little biped," Sid urged. "Come to Uncle Sid."

But Roshan didn't move in Sid's direction. Instead he wobbled over to Diego.

"No, no, no. Go to him." Diego pointed to Manfred. Just as Roshan reached the tiger, he stumbled and grabbed onto Diego's leg for support. The tiger gave in and gently raised his paw to help the baby to his feet.

"Aw, our little guy's growing up!" Sid exclaimed.

In the morning, as the weary travelers continued their journey toward Half-Peak, Diego kept a nervous eye out for the other tigers. The woolly mammoth had risked his life to save Diego. How could Diego go ahead with the plan to lead the animals into Soto's trap? He couldn't, but he didn't know how to stop it now.

"Maybe we shouldn't do this," Diego said. "If we save the kid, he'll grow up to be a hunter."

"Maybe because we saved him, he won't hunt us," Sid said.

"Yeah, and maybe he'll grow fur and a long, skinny neck and call you Mama," Diego quipped.

He let Manfred and Sid get ahead of him as he tried to figure out what to do.

Diego could see flashes of tiger fur on the next hill. "Get down!" he warned Sid and Manfred suddenly. "Follow me!"

"What's going on?" Sid asked.

"At the bottom of Half-Peak there's an ambush waiting for you," Diego admitted with honest regret. "I was supposed to get the baby, but then you . . ."

"You set us up!" Manfred exclaimed. "You brought us home for dinner!"

"That's it! You're outta the herd!" Sid added angrily.

"I'm sorry," Diego said.

Manfred charged toward the tiger and pinned him to the wall. He pressed one of his sharp tusks under Diego's chin. "You're not sorry. Not yet."

"Listen, I can help you," Diego promised. "You have to trust me."

"Trust you?" Manfred exclaimed. "Why in the world would we trust you?"

Diego looked him straight in the eye. "Because I'm your only chance."

Diego was right. Sid and Manfred would have to follow the tiger's orders and hope for the best. They hid quietly and watched as the tiger rejoined his pack.

"Diego, I was beginning to worry about you," Soto greeted him.

"I see the sloth! And he's got the baby!" Zeke exclaimed. Soto turned back to the pack. "Don't give away your positions until you see the mammoth," he ordered.

Soto's directions did not fit in with Diego's plans. He wanted the tigers to attack right away. He crept over to Zeke and whispered in his ear, "What are you waiting for? Now, Zeke, get 'em!"

Zeke bolted out from behind the rock. The others followed close behind him.

"No! I said, wait for the mammoth!" Soto shouted. But it was too late. Zeke leaped onto a bank of very deep snow and headed for the sloth. Sid slid away as fast as he could while all the tigers chased him. He was wearing skis fashioned from tree branches. One fell off, but he continued to whisk down the slope until he fell headfirst into a snowdrift, sending Roshan flying into the air.

Soto grabbed the baby. He whipped the blanket off and stared in surprise. Roshan was not there. Soto had captured a baby made of snow. Sid had tricked him!

Soto smashed the snow baby with his mighty paw and roared with anger. "Get him!"

Sid turned and grabbed Roshan, ducking just in time to see Zeke leaping at him. Zeke landed headfirst in a sheet of rock.

Meanwhile, Oscar and Lenny were headed straight toward Sid, but Manfred was ready for them. He held a large lava spike in his tusk. He swung it and whacked the tigers off the ledge.

Soto stared at Manfred, his eyes blazing. Then Diego appeared from around a bend. "C'mon, Diego," Soto called. "Let's bring this mammoth down!"

Diego blocked his way. "Leave the mammoth alone," he ordered. Soto was confused. Then he understood that Diego had deceived him.

"Fine," Soto snarled. "I'll take you down first." He leaped toward Diego. The two tigers tussled for a moment, then Soto sent Diego reeling with a punch.

Soto turned back to Manfred, stalking him. Lenny and Oscar were on their paws again and ready to help. Manfred backed away from the tigers and smacked into a rock wall with a thud. He was trapped!

Soto charged toward Manfred. But just before he reached him, Diego leaped between them to protect Manfred. As Soto's razor-sharp teeth pierced his skin, Diego fell to the ground.

Although he was growing very weak, Diego found the strength to scratch and claw at Soto furiously. Then Manfred's trunk lashed out at Soto, pushing the wild tiger against the side of the icy mountain. Soto fell onto his back. Above him a pair of enormous icicles hung from the mountain's edge. The frozen daggers loosened from the impact and fell directly onto Soto. In a moment, the evil tiger was gone forever.

Sid, Roshan, and Manfred rushed to Diego's side. Their friend was injured badly. "I'm sorry I set you up," the tiger apologized weakly. Then he glanced at Roshan. "You'll have to return the little guy without me. Once those humans get to the pass you'll never catch them," warned Diego.

"You didn't have to do that," Manfred told Diego gratefully.

Diego managed a small smile. "That's what you do in a herd." Roshan reached out and hugged him hard. After a moment Manfred placed Roshan on his back. It was time to give the boy back to his people.

Manfred spotted the humans just as they were about to enter Glacier Pass.

Sadly, Runar placed Roshan's necklace on a mound of snow before rejoining his tribe. Suddenly, Manfred and Sid were standing before him. Not sure of their intentions, Runar lifted his spear in defense.

With his trunk, Manfred grabbed the spear from Runar and tossed it to the ground. Seeing this, the other humans charged toward the mammoth, ready to attack. Then, from behind the large furry tuft on Manfred's head, Roshan's smiling face appeared. Stunned, Runar signaled for his men to fall back.

Manfred gently handed Roshan to his father and watched as Runar hugged his son. With their mission complete, it was time for Manfred and Sid to be on their way. But Roshan squealed and squirmed for his father to put him down. He waddled over to Sid and Manfred for a final hug.

"Don't forget about us, okay?" Sid said.

"We won't forget about you," Manfred promised, handing Roshan back to his father. Runar was grateful to be reunited with his son. He thanked Manfred by scooping Roshan's necklace out of the snow and gently draping it on one of the mammoth's tusks. Manfred would always treasure this special gift.

Sid wiped his eyes. "Good-bye. Good-bye," he called as he waved, practically sobbing. He watched as Roshan and Runar grew smaller and smaller in the distance. Then he noticed the child had covered his eyes and was playing peekaboo. Sid played along, trying to smile. "That's right! Where's the baby?"

"Come on, Sid. Let's head south."

As the humans vanished over the hill, Manfred turned away—and froze in his tracks. Diego was limping toward him.

"Bye," Sid said one final time.

"Save your breath, Sid. You know humans can't talk."

The sloth whirled around when he heard that familiar voice, his face lighting up with joy. "Diego! You're okay!"

"Nine lives, baby."

Sid ran to him, tackled him playfully, then planted a big kiss right on the tiger's nose.

Manfred wandered over. "Welcome back. Want a lift?"

"No, thanks. I've gotta save whatever dignity I've got left."

"I'll take that lift," Sid said hopefully to Manfred. "Pick me up, buddy! This is going to be the best winter ever. I'm telling you, I'll show you all my favorite watering holes. . . ."

Manfred wrapped his trunk around Sid and placed him on his back, then headed south with Diego loping alongside. This special herd was together again.

EPILOGUE

A tiny iceberg floated in the ocean. It carried the scrat inside, still clutching his acorn. As the icy block washed up on shore, the acorn rolled out and settled in the sand. But only briefly. A wave caught it and washed it out to sea again. The scrat let out a scream and broke free of the ice. Running blindly, he smacked right into a tree.

Surprisingly, a coconut dropped into the sand nearby. The little scrat jumped for joy. He lifted the coconut high above his head and . . . bam. He planted it in the sand with all his might. Then, suddenly, his ears began to twitch. A crack in the sand whipped up the beach, swished through the trees, seared the rocks in half, and scurried up to the summit of a dormant volcano. Ka-boom! Here we go again. . . .